3/07 J/796

ORLANDO MAGIC

RICHARD RAMBECK

COVER AND TITLE PAGE PHOTOS BY MATT MAHURIN

CREATIVE EDUCATION

Published by Creative Education, Inc.
123 S. Broad Street, Mankato, Minnesota 56001 USA

Art Director, Rita Marshall
Cover and title page photography by Matt Mahurin
Book design by Rita Marshall

Photos by: Allsport; Mel Bailey; Bettmann Archive; Brian Drake; Duomo; Focus On Sports; FPG; Photo by Sissac; South Florida Images Inc.; Spectra-Action; Sportschrome; Sports Photo Masters, Inc.; SportsLight: Brian Drake, Long Photography; Wide World Photos.

Copyright © 1993 Creative Education, Inc.
International copyrights reserved in all countries.
No part of this book may be reproduced in any form without written permission from the publisher.
Printed in the United States of America.

Library of Congress Cataloging-in-Publication Data

Rambeck, Richard.
  Orlando Magic / Richard Rambeck.
  Summary: A history of the NBA expansion team that began playing in Orlando, Florida, during the 1989-90 season.
  ISBN 0-88682-558-X

  1. Orlando Magic (Basketball team)—History—Juvenile literature. [1. Orlando Magic (Basketball team)—History. 2. Basketball—History.] I. Title.
GV885.52.O75R36 1992   92-3168
796.323'64'0975924—dc20   CIP

ORLANDO: HOME OF THE MAGIC

Located in the middle of the Florida peninsula, the city of Orlando is best known for one thing—fun. It is a city that has no trouble drawing tourists. Orlando boasts a land of magic within its borders: Walt Disney World's Magic Kingdom. It is also home to Epcot Center, Sea World, and Universal Studios, several more places where millions of people go each year to have a good time.

All of Orlando's fun and magic fill a fairly small area. In fact, Orlando is only the seventh-largest city in the state of Florida—behind Jacksonville, Miami, Tampa, St. Petersburg, Fort Lauderdale, and Hialeah. Orlando's metropolitan region is growing rapidly, however, and is already home to nearly one million people.

Magic forward Sidney Green.

On January 5, 1987, ground was broken on Orlando Arena, the home of the Magic.

During the mid-1980s, Orlando's civic leaders looked for ways to make the city more prominent. One thought was to establish a professional sports franchise in Orlando. The idea made sense. Sports and Orlando had gone hand in hand for a long time. The city has been host to a college football postseason game, now known as the Citrus Bowl, since 1947. In addition, Orlando had a franchise in the World Football League during the mid-1970s. Unfortunately, that league went out of business after only two seasons.

Also during the mid-1980s, officials of the National Basketball Association decided to expand their league. There were already 23 franchises in the NBA, and league executives wanted to add up to four more teams. Civic leaders in Orlando decided to throw the city's hat into the NBA expansion ring.

PUTTING THE MAGIC IN ORLANDO

To bring pro basketball to Orlando, city leaders hired a man with extensive knowledge of the NBA and put him in charge of the effort to secure an expansion team. His name was Pat Williams. Williams, a flamboyant personality, had spent 16 years as a general manager in the league. He was known as someone who could build teams by acquiring outstanding players and then successfully market them with outlandish promotions.

Williams started as general manager of the hapless Chicago Bulls in 1969 and turned them into a contending team during the mid-1970s. By the time the Bulls reached their peak in 1974, however, Williams was no longer with

The multitalented Jerry Reynolds.

Magic general manager Pat Williams started his sports career in 1962 as a minor league catcher in Miami.

them. He had moved on to manage the Philadelphia 76ers, who had set a single-season league record for losses just before Williams arrived.

Williams made an immediate difference in Philadelphia. He signed George McGinnis, a superstar in the American Basketball Association. Then Williams traded for Julius "Dr. J" Erving, probably the most exciting pro basketball player of the time. Suddenly the 76ers were transformed from losers to one of the best teams in the league. Williams kept the 76ers on top by signing such players as Moses Malone and Charles Barkley to Philadelphia contracts.

Williams decided to leave Philadelphia in the mid-1980s. Orlando's city leaders soon came knocking at his door. They invited Williams to become the president and general manager of an Orlando NBA team that didn't have a name yet and wasn't even assured of gaining entry into the league. He accepted the challenge. Williams moved to Florida and began working with a group of investors who planned to own the team if the NBA did indeed expand into Orlando.

Williams was the right man to "sell" the league on Orlando. Because of his years in Chicago and Philadelphia, Williams already knew the top NBA officials very well. He also believed strongly that his group had what the league was looking for. The NBA officials agreed with Williams, and in April 1987, they granted Orlando one of four expansion franchises. Two of the other expansion teams—Miami and Charlotte—would begin play in the 1988-89 season. Orlando and Minnesota would enter the league the following year.

Williams was disappointed that Orlando would have to wait another season, but he had other tasks to keep him busy. One was finding a nickname for the team. Williams wanted a name that was unique and memorable, and one that applied to Orlando. There were several under consideration, including "Heat," "Tropics," and "Juice."

The inspiration for the final decision came from an unlikely source, Williams' seven-year-old daughter, Karyn. During the formation days of the Orlando franchise, Pat Williams was separated from his family, who still lived near Philadelphia. One time, Karyn came to Florida to visit her father. The child loved the sun and heat of Orlando, not to mention Mickey Mouse and Walt Disney World. As Williams was putting his daughter on the plane for her trip home, Karyn turned to her father and said, "Daddy, it's really great down here. This place is magic." Williams made the decision that day; the team would be known as the Orlando Magic.

"Stuff, the Magic Mascot" made his first appearance on Halloween night, 1988.

MATT'S A MATCH FOR ORLANDO

With the team's nickname determined, Williams set out to hire a coach. Because Williams loved fast-breaking, high-scoring teams, he wanted someone who favored that style of play. He had a long list of candidates, but one name moved to the top. Williams called former Philadelphia coach Matt Guokas, who had recently been fired by the 76ers. Williams and Guokas had worked together for many years. In fact, Williams had hired Guokas for his first NBA coaching job—that of a 76ers assistant

Defensive standout Jeff Turner.

Terry Catledge drives to the basket.

Matt Guokas' three 76ers teams achieved a 119-88 record.

coach—several years before, and later named him Philadelphia's head coach. Guokas spent two and a half years as the Philadelphia floor general. He was fired midway through his third season, even though he had led the 76ers to the playoffs his first two years.

During their conversation, Williams asked the now-idle Guokas whether he was interested in coaching again. Williams knew that Guokas had also been mentioned as a candidate for the job at Charlotte. "If you had your choice —and I'm not saying you would have your choice—of coaching Charlotte in '88 or Orlando in '89, what would it be?" Williams inquired. "Orlando in '89," Guokas quickly replied.

Guokas decided to make an extended visit to Orlando. He soon discovered the magic of the area. "I liked the city, and I liked Florida," Guokas said. "Why? Right up there." He pointed to the sun. When Williams offered him the job, Guokas jumped at it. "The opportunity to build something in two, three, four, five years is something I thought might be fun," explained Orlando's new coach.

BUILDING THE MAGIC'S KINGDOM

Guokas may have been expecting to have fun, but he and Williams both knew it would take hard work to build a solid team in Orlando. Like the other expansion clubs, the Magic would get its players from two sources: the expansion draft and the college draft. The Magic would be able to select players from other NBA teams, each of which was allowed to protect eight players from being drafted. That meant the players the Magic would get wouldn't be stars, or even starters. Most of these players would be veterans whose best days were behind them.

Only four active NBA players had appeared in more games than Reggie Theus when he joined the Magic.

But Williams knew that sometimes NBA teams failed to protect players who still could produce. So he and Guokas spent much of the 1988-89 season studying all the teams in the NBA, looking for people likely to be available in the expansion draft. Williams also spent time examining the two expansion teams that started playing during the 1988-89 season, the Charlotte Hornets and the Miami Heat. He wanted to see how these teams built their clubs and to learn what they did right and what they did wrong.

At the same time, Williams kept a close eye on the other expansion franchise that would begin playing in 1989-90, the Minnesota Timberwolves. "We were intent on outdueling Minnesota," Williams recalled. "We'll be compared with Minnesota in our early years, and we wanted to get the jump on them quickly."

13

Even Terry Catledge's 25 points and 16 rebounds were not enough for Orlando to win its opening game in 1989.

In June 1990, Orlando and Minnesota took part in the expansion draft. Williams and Guokas wanted players who could play a fast-breaking, full-court style—players who could run and jump well. There were two veterans available in the draft whom Williams and Guokas really wanted: forward Sidney Green from the New York Knicks and guard Reggie Theus from the Atlanta Hawks. Green was a solid rebounder who could be the cornerstone of Orlando's front line. Theus was a guard who could not only score, but serve as the team's playmaker.

Williams figured his team, which was picking first in the expansion draft, would get one of the players and the Timberwolves would get the other. As it turned out, Orlando was able to select both Theus and Green when Minnesota used its first pick to take Rick Mahorn of the Detroit Pistons. "Can you believe this?" exclaimed a shocked Williams. "Hey, this is better than we could have hoped."

Orlando's luck in the draft didn't stop there, though. The Magic picked up power forward Terry Catledge from the Washington Bullets, small forward Otis Smith from the Golden State Warriors, and versatile Jerry Reynolds from the Seattle SuperSonics. As the draft moved along, Magic officials had their eyes on one other player, point guard Scott Skiles from the Indiana Pacers. "We were tempted to wait a little longer before taking Skiles, but Matty [Guokas] wouldn't hear of it," Williams recalled. "I want him on my team," Guokas insisted, "so let's not gamble."

After taking Skiles, Williams and Guokas exchanged smiles. Things had gone extremely well for their club in the expansion draft. "After this draft, we felt we had accom-

Small forward Otis Smith.

On January 30, 1990, Sam Vincent had 21 points, 17 assists, and 11 rebounds for Orlando's first "triple-double."

plished a lot by getting a mix of established pros and young prospects," Williams explained. "We also felt the pickings were better than the Miami-Charlotte [expansion] draft a year earlier."

With the expansion draft complete, Magic officials turned their attention to the college draft. Both Williams and Guokas were drooling over the prospect of drafting Nick Anderson, a high-leaping, 6-foot-6 forward from the University of Illinois. Anderson had helped lead Illinois to the 1989 NCAA Final Four and had finished second in the voting for the Big Ten's Most Valuable Player. Most pro scouts expected Anderson, a junior, to stay in school for his final year. But Anderson decided to turn pro a year early, which made a lot of Big Ten coaches happy.

"Anderson is special," said Michigan coach Steve Fisher. "He's Illinois' most dangerous player. We couldn't defend

Nick Anderson.

The Magic touch: forward Jerry Reynolds.

As a rookie, Nick Anderson ranked second on the team in shooting and third in scoring, steals, and blocks.

him. He was too quick for our big guys and too strong for our smaller guys. If I was a pro coach and could have him, I'd lick my chops." At least one NBA coach agreed with Fisher. "If I had any guts, I'd take Anderson with our pick," said San Antonio coach Larry Brown, whose team had the third selection in the draft. "That's how good I think he will be."

But San Antonio didn't take Anderson; the Spurs had their eyes on Arizona forward Sean Elliott instead. Orlando, picking eleventh in the draft, was pretty sure Anderson would already be taken by Minnesota, whose turn came just before the Magic's. But Orlando was lucky again: Minnesota decided to go with Jerome "Pooh" Richardson, a point guard from UCLA, so the Magic got their man. "We wanted Anderson so badly we could taste it," Williams said.

"We could only pray they [the Timberwolves] wouldn't take him. We couldn't believe he was still there when it was our turn to pick."

A FAST START FOR ORLANDO

With Anderson added to the solid group of veterans acquired in the expansion draft, the Magic and its fans were expecting good things from their first-year club. But nobody was counting on the kind of start the Magic had during the opening month of the 1989-90 season. Orlando won its second regular-season game November 6, 1989, against the New York Knicks, champions of the Atlantic Division the year before. Orlando beat New York 118-110 as Reggie Theus poured in 24 points.

During the 1989-90 season, Reggie Theus scored 30 or more points in eight games.

Two days after the victory over the Knicks, the Magic journeyed to Cleveland for a game with the Cavaliers, a team that had posted an impressive 57-25 record the previous season. Predictably, Orlando fell far behind, trailing by as many as 25 points in the first half. But then Theus led the team on a remarkable comeback. The 6-foot-7 sharpshooting guard scored 28 points, most of them in the second half, to lead the Magic to a 117-110 victory.

Later in November, Orlando won three straight games at home, beating Philadelphia, Sacramento, and Utah. The winning streak gave the team a lot of confidence going into a November 28 game against the Miami Heat, a contest billed as the "Battle for NBA Bragging Rights of the Sunshine State." The Magic claimed those bragging rights with a 104-98 victory, behind the 26 points of Terry Catledge and the 24 of Nick Anderson. Two days later,

Scott Skiles, the Magic floor general.

Orlando defeated fellow first-year expansion team Minnesota 103-96. What a great November that turned out to be in Orlando!

The amazing Magic had completed its first month of NBA play with a 7-7 record, the best start ever by an NBA expansion team. Orlando lost its first four games in December before playing the powerful Los Angeles Lakers at home. It was the Magic vs. Magic: Orlando vs. Earvin "Magic" Johnson, the Lakers' star guard. But the guy with the magic that night was Catledge, who scored 28 points and grabbed 12 rebounds. The Magic defeated Los Angeles and its Magic, 108-103.

Despite its great start, Orlando struggled the rest of the season, winning only 10 more games. The club's lack of inside strength and its defensive weaknesses made it difficult to stop other teams from scoring. The Magic finished with an 18-64 record, which was four games behind Minnesota's 22-60 mark.

Terry Catledge's 49 points against Golden State in January 1990 remains tops in Magic history.

SKILES AND SCOTT LEAD THE WAY

During the offseason, Pat Williams was determined to improve the Magic. His first move was to trade Theus to New Jersey for two second-round draft choices. Theus had been Orlando's second-leading scorer in 1989-90, with an 18.9 average. But Williams believed he could make the team better by trading Theus and giving more playing time to scrappy guard Scott Skiles.

Skiles had started slowly in Orlando, but he came on at the end of the 1989-90 season. Even though he wound up as Orlando's ninth-leading scorer (7.7), the fans voted him the team's Most Valuable Player. The Orlando fans loved

Left to right: Greg Kite, Jeff Turner, Morlon Wiley, Chris Corchiani.

Skiles' hustle and determination. Skiles' style of play was best summed up by Barry Cooper, a sportswriter for the *Orlando Sentinel*. "Skiles isn't happy unless he's bleeding," Cooper wrote.

But Skiles did more than bleed on the court. He also was an outstanding shooter and superb passer. "The kid can do more than score," said John Thompson, coach of Georgetown University. "He goes around and checks on his teammates and makes them better players."

Skiles' leadership abilities stemmed from his tremendous confidence. Skiles knew he was small (6-foot-1) and slow, but he also believed he could overcome his weaknesses. "I put a lot of pressure on myself," he explained. "If you don't think you're any good, you're not any good. I've always had weaknesses. Let's face it. Those guys [opponents] dwarf me. I look at it like a game. How do I trick the guy guarding me?" One of Skiles' tricks was always playing at full speed. He propelled his small body up and down the court like a race car, making him the perfect guard to lead Guokas' run-and-gun offense.

But the Magic needed to add more guns to go with Skiles' running. Orlando found one of those weapons in the 1990 NBA draft. The Magic had the third pick in the draft, following New Jersey and Seattle. Again, like the year before when Nick Anderson was the apple of Williams' eye, the Magic had one player in mind. He was Dennis Scott, a 6-foot-5 guard/forward from Georgia Tech.

There were a lot of similarities between Anderson and Scott. Like Anderson, Scott was leaving school after his junior year. Also, like Anderson, Scott had led his team to the Final Four. During the 1990 NCAA tournament, Scott averaged an amazing 30.6 points a game. In the regional

During 1990-91, Scott Skiles proved he could shoot as well as pass, scoring 20 or more points 40 times.

The high-scoring Dennis Scott (pages 26-27).

championship game, he scored 40 points against the University of Minnesota, propelling Georgia Tech to a victory and a spot in the Final Four. Scott was named NCAA Player of the Year by *The Sporting News.* He was also selected Player of the Year in the Atlantic Coast Conference.

Scott was a big, physical guard who could score consistently from as far away as 30 feet. To make sure he got Scott, Williams engineered a complicated deal with New Jersey and Seattle. As part of the deal, both New Jersey and Seattle agreed not to take Scott. In return, Orlando gave both teams second-round draft picks. "We didn't want to take any chances," Williams explained. "A Dennis Scott comes along once in the life of a franchise. If you have a chance to get him, you had better react."

Rookie Dennis Scott showed his long-range ability by canning three-point shots in 12 straight games.

When the draft began, New Jersey took Syracuse forward Derrick Coleman, and then Seattle selected Oregon State point guard Gary Payton. The Magic picked Scott, and the celebration began. When Scott appeared at a press conference held at the Orlando airport after the draft, hundreds of fans jammed one of the airport's concourses, closing it down. While the fans screamed and the Magic cheerleaders danced, a band played "Happy Days Are Here Again."

Those happy days continued after the 1990-91 season began. The second-year Magic proved to be the most improved team in the NBA, winning 13 more games than it had the previous season. Scott Skiles was the driving force behind the Magic's success. He led the team in scoring (17.2) and assists (8.4). For his efforts, Skiles was named the NBA's Most Improved Player of the Year.

Skiles' remarkable season included a performance that made history. On December 30, 1990, he handed out 30

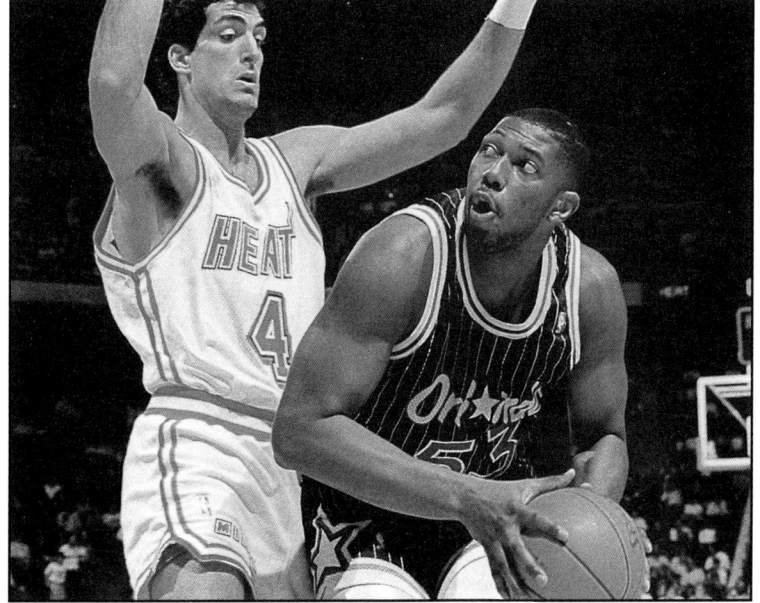

Stanley Roberts was the Magic's top reserve in 1991-92, averaging 10 points and 6 rebounds per game.

assists in Orlando's victory over Denver, breaking an NBA record that had stood for more than 15 years. "Scott deserves a lot of credit for the way he spreads the floor, creating opportunities for his teammates," said Magic coach Matt Guokas. "That's why he's one of the better point guards in the league."

But Skiles wasn't the only reason the Magic, finishing 31-51, posted the best record among the four expansion teams in 1990-91. Rookie Dennis Scott was second on the team in scoring with a 15.7 average. The long-range bomber was also fourth in the league in number of three-point shots made. Scott's fine play earned him a spot on the NBA's All-Rookie first team.

The Magic also got solid years from Terry Catledge and Nick Anderson, even though both missed a lot of games because of injuries. Catledge averaged 14.6 points and

High-flying forward Michael Ansley.

Future NBA superstar Shaquille O'Neal.

Magic fans cheered their first All-Star, Scott Skiles, during the 1992 classic held in Orlando Arena.

almost seven rebounds a game. Anderson chipped in 14.1 points and 5.5 rebounds a contest.

Thanks to the efforts of these players, the Magic posted a 17-18 record after the All-Star Game in 1990-91. "We're going to pick up right where we left off," said forward Mark Acres, predicting great things for the team in the 1990s.

LOOKING AHEAD

In order to make Mark Acres' prediction of success come true, the Magic will need to improve in the areas of rebounding and defense. The team added plenty of height and muscle in the first round of the 1991 college draft by taking 6-foot-10 forward Brian Williams from Arizona and 7-foot center Stanley Roberts, who went to Louisiana State and then spent a year playing in Spain. If the Magic is to continue to improve, Williams and Roberts must develop quickly. Roberts, in particular, is considered a raw talent with a lot of potential. "If he makes it," Pat Williams said of Roberts, "he's a big-time talent."

Coach Guokas believes the team is strong at guard (with Scott Skiles and Nick Anderson) and small forward (with Dennis Scott and Jerry Reynolds). The key to success is adding strength to speed and shooting. "I hope I can continue to mold our talented group of individuals into a team which will accept the demands of being a competitive unit every game," Guokas said.

Further down the road, hopes are high for bringing an NBA championship to the city best known as the home of Walt Disney World's Magic Kingdom. If that NBA title dream does come true, then Orlando might become known as the city of the *Magic's* Kingdom.